W9-BWO-091

This is the story of
how young Zeus, with a little
help from six monsters, five gods
(his brothers and sisters), his mother,
and an enchanted she-goat (that's me!),
became god of gods, master of lightning
and thunder, and ruler over all.

CAST OF CHARACTERS

ZEUS (ZOOse), the young god

GAIA (GUY-uh), Zeus's grandmother (the earth)

URANUS (you-RAY-nus), Zeus's grandfather (the sky)

RHEA (RAY-uh), Zeus's mother, a Titan (TIE-tuhn)

CRONUS (CROW-nus), Zeus's father, another Titan

the rest of the TITANS

the CYCLOPES (SY-kloh-peez)

the HUNDRED-HANDERS

HERA (HARE-uh), DEMETER (dee-MEE-tur),
HESTIA (HESS-tee-uh), HADES (HAY-deez), and
POSEIDON (po-SY-din), Zeus's brothers and sisters

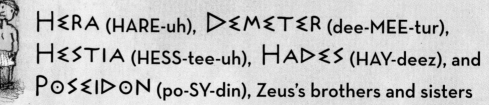

...and AMALTHEIA (ah-MAL-thee-uh), the enchanted she-goat

YOUNG ZEUS

BY G. BRIAN KARAS

SCHOLASTIC PRESS · NEW YORK

AUTHOR'S NOTE

I've wanted to work with myths for a long time but didn't feel a personal connection to any in particular. Until I went to Greece. Here lived my ancestors in the lands where ancient gods and goddesses once ruled. In fact, when I learned how humanlike the deities were believed to be (flawed but lovable), I immediately recognized my relatives in all of them! I had found my personal connection.

Throughout my research I kept looking for the earliest accounts, and so largely drew from Hesiod's *Theogony* and *The Library of Apollodorus*. There I found much written about Zeus's reign as ruler of heaven and earth but very little about his boyhood. I began with those sources and, true to the nature of myths, imagined the rest. *Young Zeus* is my account of how things might have been for Zeus in those in-between years — from infancy to being the most powerful god of ancient Greece.

FOR MY FATHER

Colossal thank-yous to David Saylor and Leslie Budnick,
and to Violet for noticing all the details.

Copyright © 2010 by G. Brian Karas

All rights reserved. Published by Scholastic Press, an imprint of Scholastic Inc., *Publishers since 1920*. SCHOLASTIC, SCHOLASTIC PRESS, and associated logos are trademarks and/or registered trademarks of Scholastic Inc. No part of this publication may be reproduced, stored in a retrieval system, or transmitted in any form or by any means, electronic, mechanical, photocopying, recording, or otherwise, without written permission of the publisher. For information regarding permission, write to Scholastic Inc., Attention: Permissions Department, 557 Broadway, New York, NY 10012.

Library of Congress Cataloging-in-Publication Data is available: 2009010148
ISBN: 978-0-439-72806-5
Printed in Singapore   46
12 11 10 9 8 7 6 5 4 3 2   10 11 12 13 14
First edition, February 2010

The text type was set in 15-point NeutraText Demi.
The artwork was created with gouache and pencil on Canson Ingres paper.
Book design by David Saylor and Charles Kreloff

ON A NIGHT LONG, LONG AGO,

Rhea gave her baby Zeus to Amaltheia, the enchanted she-goat, who lived in a cave on the peaceful island of Crete.

"Please care for my son," Rhea whispered. "Keep him safe, hidden from his evil father, Cronus."

"Of course," said Amaltheia.

With a hug and a kiss for her baby boy, Rhea said good-bye, afraid she might never see young Zeus again.

On Crete, Zeus lived in golden sunshine, friend of beasts and birds, unaware of the danger should his father discover him.

One evening, when Zeus was no bigger than an oak tree, he asked, "Ammy, why are there no other gods to play with?"

"It's complicated," said Amaltheia. "Sit down and have some milk and honey. The trouble started with your grandfather, Uranus.

"He and your grandmother, Gaia, had many children. Twelve were magnificent giants, the Titans. They were your grandfather's pride and joy. But six were monsters! Three of them, the Cyclopes, had only one eye. And three, the Hundred-Handers, had fifty heads and one hundred arms! Your grandfather was so ashamed of these children that he locked them in the underworld forever.

"Your grandmother was furious!

"'Cronus, my son,' she commanded, 'cast your father from his throne!'
She handed him a sickle. 'Then free the Cyclopes and Hundred-Handers
from the underworld.'

"Cronus banished his father to the bottom of the sea. But he didn't complete his task. No he did not. He left the Cyclopes and Hundred-Handers to suffer in the underworld and took the throne for himself. By then, Cronus was so powerful that your grandmother couldn't get him to do *anything*.

"Still, Cronus had one weakness — the fear of being overthrown by one of his own children. To make sure that could never happen, he ate up all his babies. He swallowed them whole, and there your sisters and brothers remain, trapped inside his belly.

"And that's why there are no other gods or goddesses for you to play with," said Amaltheia.

"But . . . but —" began Zeus.

"No buts. Just good-night kisses and sweet dreams."

Years went by. Zeus grew strong and happy . . .

. . . but also troubled by dark thoughts of his cruel father, Cronus. Zeus knew one thing for sure — he had to free his brothers and sisters. But how?

As often as possible, Zeus's mother, Rhea, secretly visited to check on him. On one such day, Rhea and Amaltheia were talking when a rumble as mighty as ten earthquakes shook the ground.

In a terrible mood, Zeus had lifted a mountaintop and thrown it into the sea. "Heavens!" cried Rhea. "It's time Zeus and I had a talk."

"Who are *you*?" he asked.
"I'm your mother," said Rhea.
"Give me a hug."

But Zeus did not hug his mother.

"You missed all my birthdays!" said Zeus.

"I was here for every one," said Rhea. "You just couldn't see me."

Zeus thought for a moment, then asked the question that had been on his mind for so long.

"Why didn't my father swallow me?"

"Because I outsmarted him. When you were born, I wrapped a stone in your blanket and said, 'Here is your son.' Your father grabbed the bundle and swallowed it whole. He still thinks it's you in his belly."

"Wow . . ." said Zeus.

They hugged.

"What is it you want more than anything in the world?" asked his mother.

"To play with my brothers and sisters," said Zeus.

"Maybe I can help." Rhea handed Zeus a small vial of murky liquid and they came up with a plan.

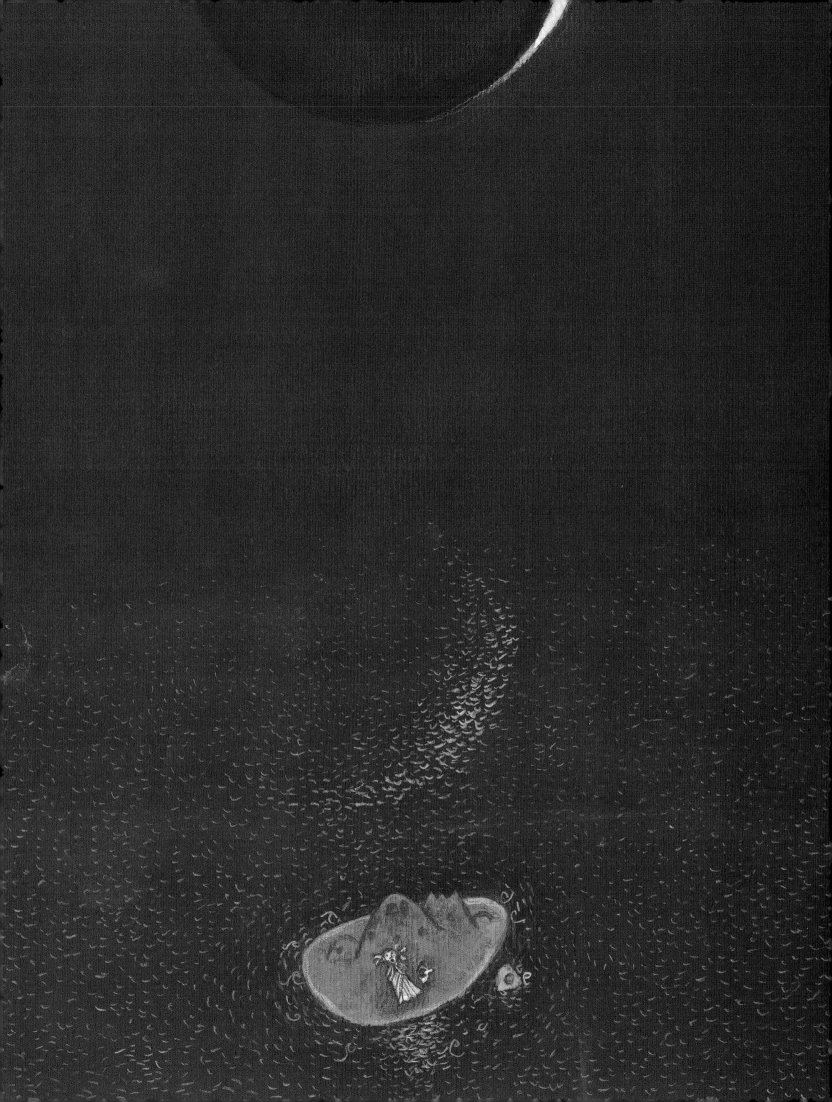

In the dark of night, Zeus set out to find his father.
"Before you go, take this honey," said Amaltheia.
"And remember," Rhea warned. "Keep your eye on Cronus. He's a sneak. And so are his brothers and sisters, the Titans. If they find out what you're up to, they will be boiling mad."

Zeus wandered through strange mists and unfamiliar lands. Fearful thoughts crept into his mind. *What if the potion doesn't work? What if Cronus finds me before I find him? What if he tries to eat me?*

Just then Zeus heard rumbling. He smelled something bad.
The fog lifted and there lay Cronus, asleep.

Without a moment to lose,
Zeus poured the foul brew down
his father's throat, and as he did
he sang a song:

One-two, three-four-five,
You swallowed my brothers
*   and sisters alive.*
Now drink this stuff — set them free!
For I am ZEUS, you didn't eat me!

At once a deadly grip locked
around Zeus's neck. He choked and
wheezed. The potion had failed!

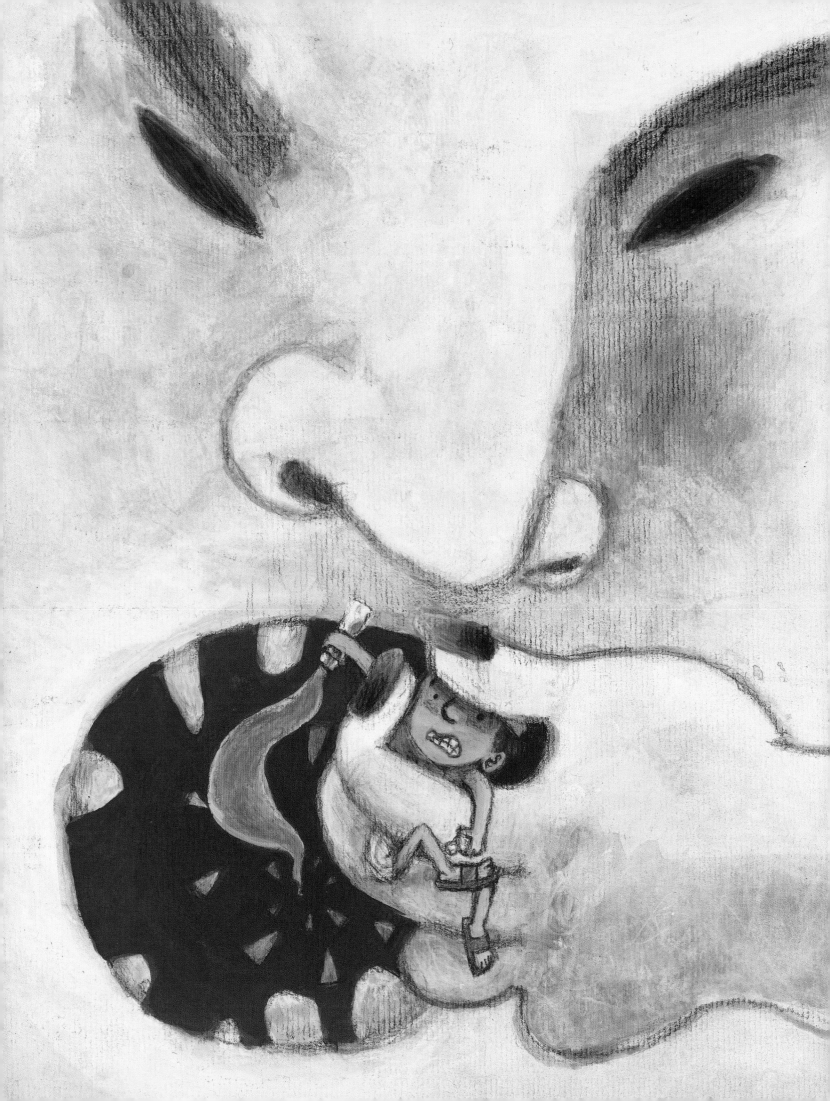

Suddenly, the ground trembled and Cronus belched. Out came the stone and blanket. Then out came Zeus's brothers and sisters — looking surprisingly good — five gods and goddesses of radiant beauty.

"I'm Zeus, your brother," said the victorious young god. "Let's play!"
"Yes!" said his brothers and sisters. "But first things first." They
pounced on Cronus. "Take that!" they cried, and threw him into the sea.

The gods and goddesses embraced Zeus.

"I am Hestia, your oldest sister, so I'm in charge."

"I am Demeter, your next oldest sister. And no, she is not."

"Ignore them! I am Poseidon, your oldest brother, therefore I am supreme ruler."

"And I am Hades, your next oldest brother, and —"

"I'm Hera," interrupted Hera. "Youngest sister but still older than you."

The gods and goddesses bickered, unaware of a towering shadow darkening the land. Ten giants filled the sky. Zeus remembered his mother's warning. . . .

"The Titans! The Titans!" shouted Zeus. "Stop arguing! Let's get 'em!"

But no one listened to Zeus.
"Look at the mess you got us into!" yelled Hestia.
"You started it!" snapped Demeter.
Poseidon and Hades growled at each other, and
Hera bossed Zeus around.
All seemed lost.

Then Zeus heard a voice from the earth beneath his feet.
"Zeus, it's your grandmother, Gaia. If you can free the Cyclopes and
Hundred-Handers from the underworld, they will help you. Quick. Go!"

So Zeus traveled down, down, down through three layers of night, to below the very bottom of the earth, and in the gloom found the underworld.

A dragon kept watch over the prisoners. "What's this?" asked the dragon. "A sweet meaty treat?" Her forked tongue slithered like a hungry snake toward Zeus.

Zeus quickly came up with a song:

Dragon, dragon, fearsome beast,
Don't eat me, for I'm no feast.
If sweet is what you like to eat,
Have some honey.
It's yum-yum-yummy!

This particular dragon had a weakness for sweets. As she slurped, Zeus tiptoed toward the gates.

"Cyclopes and Hundred-Handers! I'm your nephew Zeus, here to set you free!" He flung open the gates.

"Hail, Zeus!" They wept with joy.

"Dear Uncles, join me in the battle with the Titans."

"Say no more," they cried. "To war!"

The Cyclopes gave Zeus a bundle of thunderbolts.
"A gift for mighty Zeus!" they cheered, and off they flew.

The gods and goddesses were almost done in by the time Zeus returned.

"What took so long?" cried Hestia.

"What's the use?" wailed Demeter. "All is lost!"

"You're always so negative," said Poseidon.

"And you're always so critical!" said Hades.

"ZEUS!" yelled Hera. "DO SOMETHING!!!"

From the highest mountaintop, Zeus hurled bolt after bolt of his mighty lightning at the Titans. "Go away! Let us play!" he thundered. The earth quaked. The sky was on fire. Bolt after mighty bolt rained upon the Titans.

When at last all fell silent, Zeus sighed a sigh that filled the land. The battle was over. The defeated Titans were cast into the underworld.

"Thank heavens!" Gaia's voice rang from the scorched earth. To the Cyclopes and Hundred-Handers she commanded, "Live where you wish." To the gods and goddesses she said, "Go home to Mount Olympus." And they did.

Right from the start, there was disagreement.

"Play first, chores later," said Hestia.

"Chores first, then play," said Demeter.

"No! No!" said Poseidon.

"Yes! Yes!" said Hades.

"I'm hungry," said Hera.

"Enough!" shouted Zeus. "From now on, we do things *my* way."

"Who made you boss?" they all yelled.

"I did!" said Zeus.

The earth grumbled. Gaia spoke. "Listen to your brother."

It was settled. Young Zeus became ruler of heaven and earth.
He divided up chores and scheduled playtimes. His mother,
Rhea, was so proud.
    And thus began fun and order on Mount Olympus.

So ends the tale of how young Zeus became ruler over all. And with his family by his side, he reigned supreme for ages to come.

PL
820
.58
K43
2010